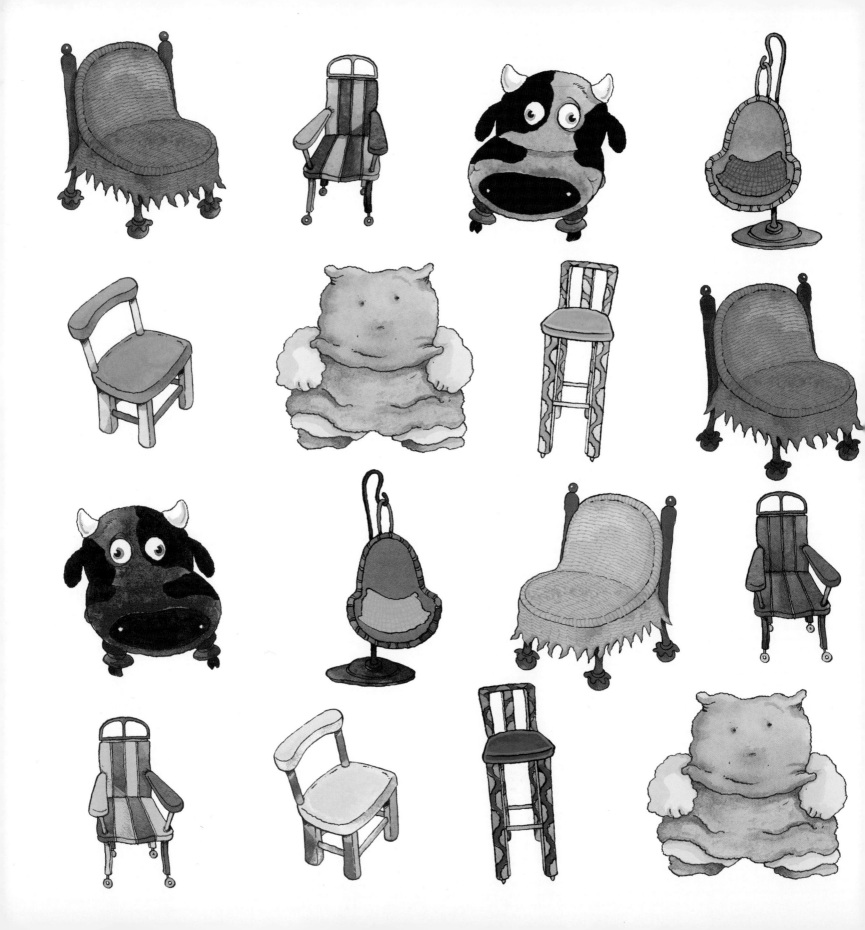

For Vineeta – K.U.

For Chris, with love
– C.F.

OXFORD
UNIVERSITY PRESS

Great Clarendon Street, Oxford OX2 6DP

Oxford University Press is a department of the University of Oxford.
It furthers the University's objective of excellence in research, scholarship,
and education by publishing worldwide in

Oxford New York

Auckland Cape Town Dar es Salaam Hong kong Karachi
Kuala Lumpur Madrid Melbourne Mexico City Nairobi
New Delhi Shanghai Taipei Toronto
With offices in
Argentina Austria Brazil Chile Czech Republic France Greece
Guatemala Hungary Italy Japan Poland Portugal Singapore
South Korea Switzerland Thailand Turkey Ukraine Vietnam

Oxford is a registered trade mark of Oxford University Press
in the UK and in certain other countries

British Library Cataloguing in Publication Data available

ISBN-13: 978-0-19-272535-6
ISBN-10: 0-19-272535-1

3 5 7 9 10 8 6 4

Originated by Dot Gradations Ltd, UK

Printed in China

A Chair for Baby Bear

Kaye Umansky   Chris Fisher

OXFORD
UNIVERSITY PRESS

"When are you going to mend my chair, Dad?" asked Baby Bear.

"Soon, Baby Bear," said Father Bear.

"You said that yesterday," said Baby Bear. "And the day before. And the day before that."

"He's right, dear," said Mother Bear. "That naughty Goldilocks broke Baby Bear's Chair a very long time ago."

"Well, all right," said Father Bear. "I think we'd better look for a new chair in Bear Town."

"Hooray!" cheered Baby Bear. "Can we go now?"

The Three Bears set off through the woods. Baby Bear played in the leaves.

"Look at me!" he shouted. "I'm Robin Hood!"

"Don't get muddy," said Father Bear.

"Can I have a Robin Hood chair?" begged Baby Bear. "Please,

please,

please?"

"We'll see," said Mother Bear.

The Three Bears came to a stream.

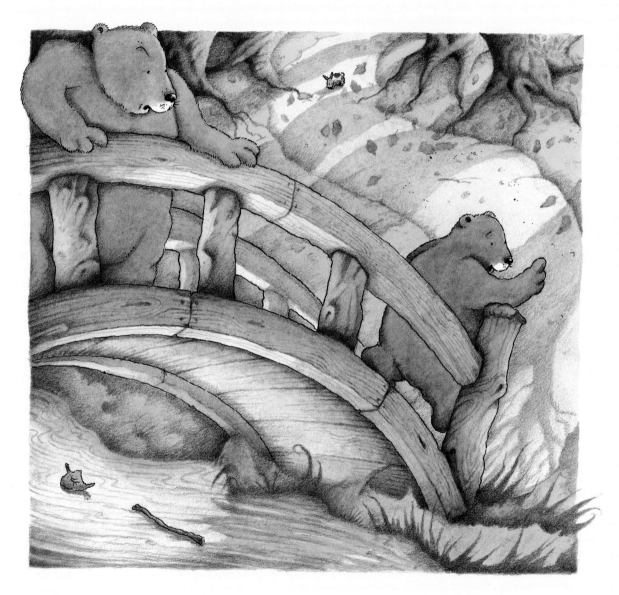

"Look at me!" cried Baby Bear.
"I'm a pirate!"

"Be careful," said Father Bear. "You'll get wet."

"Can I have a pirate chair?"
begged Baby Bear.

"Please,

please,

please?"

"We'll see," said Mother Bear.

The road wound its way around the hill. In the distance stood a grand castle. Baby Bear climbed on a rock.

"I'm the king of the castle!" he shouted.
"Mind you don't fall," said Father Bear.

"Can I have a king's chair?"
begged Baby Bear.
"Please, please, please?"

"We'll see," said Mother Bear.

All the way to Bear Town, Baby Bear thought and thought about the kind of chair he wanted.

When they reached the chair shop, he ran round and round in the revolving doors.

"Stop that at once!" cried Father Bear. "You'll make yourself sick."

In the shop, there were lots ... and lots ...

and lots ... of chairs.

There was a Robin Hood chair.
But it was much

TOO SCRATCHY.

There was a Pirate Chair.

But it was much

too scary.

There was a King's Chair. But it was much too grand. The cushion was so big and soft that when Baby Bear sat on it, he sank

down, down, down.

"Don't you like any of them?"
asked Mother Bear.

"Ye~e~ss," said Baby Bear.
"But none of them is
quite right."

"Sorry, Baby Bear," said Father Bear.
"Come on. We'd best be
going home."

Baby Bear was so disappointed. He was tired, too. So Father Bear gave him a piggyback ride all the way home.

"What's this?" said Mother Bear,
as they reached the front door.

There was a big parcel
wrapped in brown
paper sitting on the step.

Baby Bear didn't feel tired any more.
He ripped off the paper, opened the box

and...

. . . lifted out the most perfect
Little Red Bear Chair!

With it, was a note from Goldilocks.

Dear Baby Bear,

Sorry I broke your chair.

love, Goldilocks

Baby Bear tried it out.
"Hooray!" cried Baby Bear.

"It's not too scratchy,
it's not too scary and it's not too grand.

In fact, it's just right."

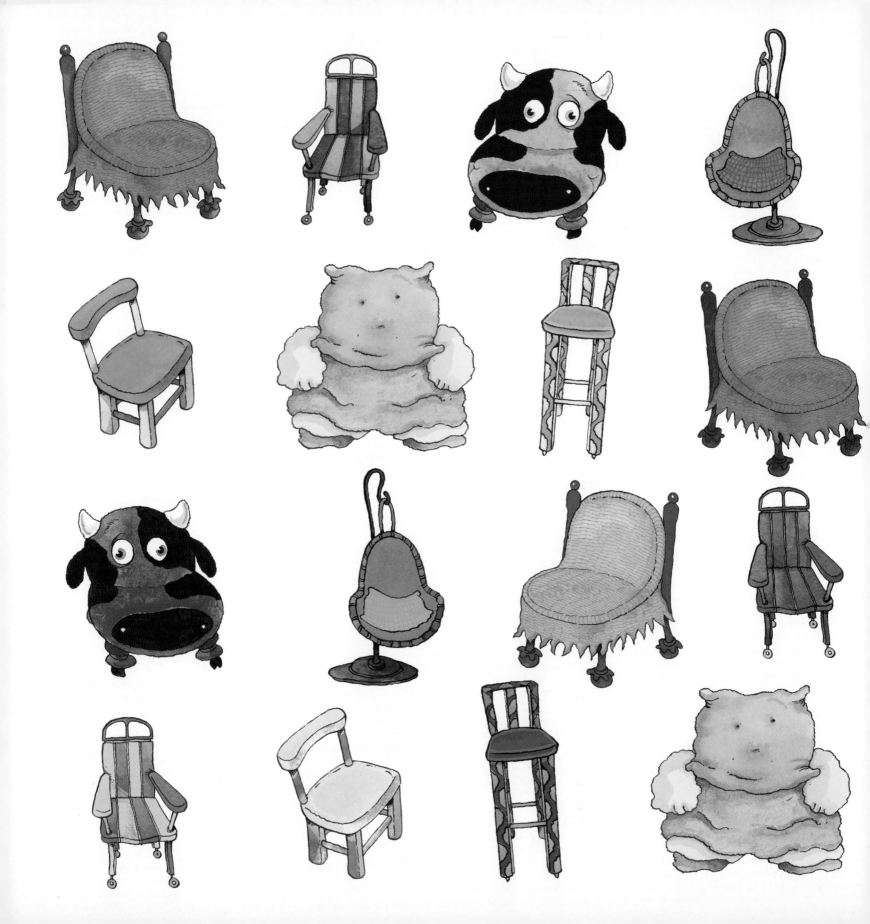